Dear Parents,

Welcome to the Scholastic Reader series. We have taken over 80 years of experience with teachers, parents, and children and put it into a program that is designed to match your child's interests and skills.

Level 1—Short sentences and stories made up of words kids can sound out using their phonics skills and words that are important to remember.

Level 2—Longer sentences and stories with words kids need to know and new "big" words that they will want to know.

Level 3—From sentences to paragraphs to longer stories, these books have large "chunks" of texts and are made up of a rich vocabulary.

Level 4—First chapter books with more words and fewer pictures.

It is important that children learn to read well enough to succeed in school and beyond. Here are ideas for reading this book with your child:

- Look at the book together. Encourage your child to read the title and make a prediction about the story.
- Read the book together. Encourage your child to sound out words when appropriate. When your child struggles, you can help by providing the word.
- Encourage your child to retell the story. This is a great way to check for comprehension.
- Have your child take the fluency test on the last page to check progress.

Scholastic Readers are designed to support your child's efforts to learn how to read at every age and every stage. Enjoy helping your child learn to read and love to read.

> **—Francie Alexander**
> Chief Education Officer
> Scholastic Education

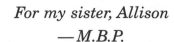

For my sister, Allison
— M.B.P.

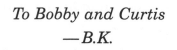

To Bobby and Curtis
— B.K.

ISBN 0-439-59889-3

Text copyright © 2004 by Marjorie Blain Parker.
Illustrations copyright © 2004 by Bob Kolar.
All rights reserved. Published by Scholastic Inc.
SCHOLASTIC, CARTWHEEL BOOKS, and associated logos
are trademarks and/or registered trademarks of Scholastic Inc.

Library of Congress Cataloging-in-Publication Data
Parker, Marjorie Blain.
  Hello, school bus! / by Marjorie Blain Parker ; illustrated by Bob
Kolar.
     p. cm. -- (Scholastic reader. Level 1)
"Cartwheel books is a trademark of Scholastic, Inc."
Summary: Easy-to-read, rhyming text celebrates a bouncing, noisy ride to
school.
  ISBN 0-439-59889-3 (pbk.)
  [1. School buses--Fiction. 2. Stories in rhyme.] I. Kolar, Bob, ill.
II. Title. III. Series.
  PZ8.3.P1695He 2004
  [E]--dc22
                                    2003015823

Hello, School Bus!

by **Marjorie Blain Parker**

Illustrated by **Bob Kolar**

Scholastic Reader — Level 1

SCHOLASTIC INC.

New York Toronto London Auckland Sydney
Mexico City New Delhi Hong Kong Buenos Aires

We wave.
We meet.
We watch and wait.

Yes! Here it comes!
We won't be late.

Hello, school bus!

Lights flash. Cars stop.

Doors open wide.

The driver smiles.
"Come on inside!"

3

The bus is big,

yellow, and black.

We climb the steps.

We walk to the back.

**Doors shut. Brakes hiss.
"Quick! Grab a seat!"**

Ready, set, go!
We roll down the street.

Wheels bump. Kids bounce

There's lots of noise!

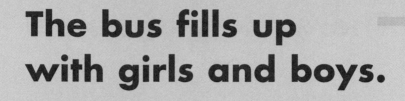

The bus fills up with girls and boys.

We play. We joke.

We sing and shout.

We are at school.
It's time to get out.

Good-bye, school bus!

Fluency Fun

The words in each list below end in the same sounds.
Read the words in a list.
Read them again.
Read them faster.
Try to read all 12 words in one minute.

be	back	hop
he	pack	mop
me	sack	top
we	black	stop

Look for these words in the story.

school   **and**   **come**

the   **down**